This igloo book belongs to:

....

igloobooks

Published in 2013
by Igloo Books Ltd
Cottage Farm
Sywell
NN6 0BJ
www.igloobooks.com

SHE001 0913
2 4 6 8 10 9 7 5 3 1
ISBN: 978-1-78197-746-0

Printed and manufactured in China

Bedtime
Stories
for Girls

igloobooks

Contents

The Magic Mirror

Once upon a time, there were three sisters who lived with their godmother in a tumbledown cottage. The two younger sisters, Constance and Clementine, were always arguing with each other and making mischief. Their older sister, Clara, spent all her time trying to teach them to be good.

One day, the sisters' godmother called them into her parlour. "You are all old enough to know the truth now," she said. "I am a good fairy who swore to take care of you after your parents died. I am your fairy godmother and I have a special gift for you."

The three sisters watched in amazement as their godmother showed them a beautiful mirror with a delicate, silver frame and a strange, murky surface. "This is a magic mirror," said the fairy godmother. "Any girl who looks into it will see the man she will one day marry."

The girls were all very excited. "Let me try it!" cried Clementine, grabbing the mirror. She gazed into it and saw herself with a poor soldier. His clothes were ragged and his sword was rusty. He was begging for money by the roadside.

Clementine laughed. "I would never marry such a man!" she scoffed. "Why, I have a grand duke who is in love with me. I will marry him."

Sure enough, some time later, Clementine did marry the duke. However, her new husband loved to gamble. One night, he bet all his money, his great house and his land, on a roll of the dice. The duke's luck was poor and he lost everything. He had to become a soldier again and he and Clementine were forced to beg for money in the streets, just as the mirror had shown.

Meanwhile, Constance had also looked in the mirror. It showed her living in the house of a poor shoemaker. "I don't think so!" said Constance. "A fine earl wants to marry me, not some silly shoemaker."

Constance was worried by what the mirror had shown her, so she married the earl as soon as she could. The day after their wedding, the earl brought Constance to a tiny shop in the middle of town. All kinds of shoes were in the window. "I am only a poor shoemaker," he said. "I told you I was an earl to get you to marry me."

Constance was very angry at her lying husband. "You rogue!" she cried and chased him around his shoemaker's shop. The magic mirror had shown the truth and Constance had to live as the wife of the poor shoemaker.

The eldest sister, Clara, hadn't looked in the mirror. She loved a woodcutter, who lived in a small cottage in the middle of the forest. He brought firewood to their godmother's house every day and he always remembered to pick a bunch of flowers for Clara.

One day, Clara was curious to see if she would indeed marry the woodcutter. She picked up the mirror and stared into it. The mirror showed a vision of Clara in a sparkling wedding dress, walking down the halls of a magnificent palace, where a handsome prince lived.

"That can't be right," Clara said. "I want to marry the woodcutter, not a prince. I don't care how rich he is, or how big his palace is. It's the woodcutter I love."

The fairy godmother had been watching Clara. "The mirror never lies," she said. "Do what your heart tells you and everything will be all right."

Soon, the woodcutter asked for Clara's hand in marriage. "I do not have much money," he said. "I am afraid that your life will be a hard one." "I have your heart," said Clara, "and that's all the treasure I need." She tried not to think about the picture she had seen in the mirror.

"Come with me," said the woodcutter, smiling. Instead of taking her to his cottage in the middle of the woods, he took her down a different path. At the end of it, a fine carriage was waiting for them.

The woodcutter pulled off his worn-out rags to reveal fine garments underneath. He helped Clara to climb into the carriage and it took them far away, to an enormous palace. "I am a prince," explained the woodcutter, "but all the fine ladies I met only liked me for my riches. I pretended to be a woodcutter to find a girl who was pure of heart. When I met you, I knew that you were that girl."

Clara was overjoyed. She would have been happy with the woodcutter, no matter what, but finding out that he was a prince made her happier still. The mirror had shown the truth, after all. "If only my family were here," Clara sighed sadly.

The next day, three carriages rolled up to the palace, which was beautifully decorated for the wedding. Constance and her shoemaker husband were in one carriage, Clementine and her soldier were in another and the fairy godmother was in the third.

"You must all come and live with us," announced the prince. "We have all the riches that you need." Everyone rejoiced, they were happy to accept the prince's generosity.

Clara and the prince had a magnificent wedding. None of the sisters ever needed to look in the magic mirror again because each one of them had found perfect happiness.

The Tortoise and the Hare

One fine day in spring, the animals of the meadow were playing in the sunshine, when a slick, speedy hare bounded up to them. The hare was very proud of how fast he could run and wanted to show off to all the other animals. He ran round the old bear from the woods, raced past the rabbits and outran the swift, sly fox.

"I'm the fastest creature in the world," said the hare, proudly. "No one can beat me." He kicked his heels up and raced round and round, so that all the animals could see him, then he stood on the meadow path and smiled smugly.

The hare was just thinking about how marvellous he was, when a small voice spoke behind him. Turning around, the hare saw an old tortoise. His shell was worn with age and he used a gnarled old twig as a walking stick. "Excuse me," said the tortoise. "Would you mind moving out of the way? My old legs aren't what they used to be."

The hare looked the old tortoise up and down. "I am the fastest animal in the world," he said. "Why should I move out of the way for a slow, old tortoise like you?"

The tortoise thought for a minute. "If you won't move," he croaked, narrowing his dark eyes, "perhaps you'd like to have a race?"
The hare laughed so much, he nearly fell over. "I would cross the finishing line before you even took your first step," he said.

"Nevertheless," said the tortoise, nodding. "I suggest we race up the old hill. The animal that reaches the top first, will be forever known as the fastest animal in the world."

"Agreed!" said the hare. Then, without waiting for another word from the tortoise, the hare sped off in the direction of the hill.

The hare ran faster than ever, across the green meadow. Before long, he had reached the steep slopes of the hill and began to bound up them. The hare looked behind him, but couldn't see the tortoise. "How will he know I'm winning?" he thought. "I have so much time, I'm going to go back and tell that tortoise how fast I am!" With that, the hare raced back down the hill.

Right near the start of the race, the tortoise was still plodding slowly along. "Ha!" panted the hare. "I am so fast that I have come back to tell you that I almost reached the top of the hill."

"Almost reaching the top of the hill doesn't make you a winner," wheezed the old tortoise and he continued to plod along, one slow step at a time.

The hare raced back to the hill. He was so sure of his success that he started leaping high in the air. "If I do this, that silly old tortoise is bound to see how far ahead I am," said the hare. He even stopped to tell all the woodland creatures about the race. "I have so much time," said the hare, "I can do whatever I want and still win!"

The hare spent so much time showing off to all the other animals, that he was beginning to feel tired. He tried to bound up the hill, but this time, because the hare had been running all day, it wasn't so easy.

The proud hare refused to climb the hill slowly. "I'm the fastest animal in the world," he thought. "I can run straight up this hill." Instead of climbing the hill bit by bit, the hare charged upwards, using up most of his energy. When he finally reached the top, he was exhausted. Just up ahead was the tree that marked the finishing line.

"I'm so tired," yawned the hare. He looked down the hill, but the old tortoise was nowhere to be seen. "I'm still so far ahead, it can't hurt to take a little nap," he said, sleepily. So the hare lay down on the cool grass and fell fast asleep.

Meanwhile, the old tortoise plodded on and on, never speeding up, but never slowing down, either. He just kept going at his own tortoise pace.

At the top of the hill, the hare slept for hours and hours. When he woke, the sun was almost setting. "How silly of me," said the hare, yawning and rubbing his eyes. "I've got a race to win."

The hare looked up towards the tree at the top of the hill and couldn't believe his eyes. The tortoise was about to cross the finishing line.

Determined not to be beaten by an old, slow tortoise, the hare shot off like a flash towards the tree. He tore through the grass, jumped through the ferns, then tripped and fell head-first into a thorn bush. The hare rolled out of the thorn bush and scrambled across to the tree, only to find that it was too late. The tortoise had won the race!

A crowd of cheering animals surrounded the tortoise. "Well done," said the badger. "You are the winner of this race and therefore, the fastest animal in the world."

When the hare heard this, he stared with his mouth open. Then he began to laugh. Soon the tortoise was laughing too and before long, all the other animals joined in. "I'm sorry I was so rude to you," said the hare to the tortoise. "I was so busy showing off and telling everyone how fast I was, I used up all my energy. But you just kept going and going and you won the race, fair and square."

The tortoise smiled wisely. "Sometimes, slow and steady is best," he said. The hare agreed and from that day on, he became a lot less boastful and proud. Whenever he felt the need to show off, the hare remembered how the tortoise had won the race.

As for the tortoise, it took him a long time to plod all the way home, but he smiled every slow step of the way.

The Genie of the Teapot

Long ago, in ancient Arabia, there lived two brothers named Ali and Haroun. The brothers were orphans and lived on the streets of a great city, running errands and begging for money. Sometimes, they would walk around the walls of the sultan's palace, looking for food. Ali and Haroun would stare up at the huge turrets and dream of the riches that must lie inside the palace.

One night, Ali and Haroun were very hungry. They sat in the bazaar, near the palace, hoping to get some scraps of food. Suddenly, Ali noticed a shaft of golden light streaming from an open door. Beyond the doorway, he could see a room full of food. There were piles of sweets and pastries, rich desserts and mouth-watering roast meats. Ali realised that he was looking into the kitchen of the palace.

Ali was so hungry, he forgot all about Haroun and stepped inside the kitchen. No one seemed to be around, so Ali reached for the nearest morsel of food. Before he could take a single bite, he heard a loud cry. "Stop, thief!" shouted the palace cook and grabbed Ali's arm. "You must come with me to the sultan," growled the cook. "He will punish you!"

The cook marched Ali to the Great Hall. The sultan sat on a gigantic cushion, surrounded by slaves and courtiers. One slave fanned him with a palm leaf, while another fed him from a dish, piled high with sweets. All around the hall there were beautiful, sparkling jewels.

Ali had to wait in a long line of scared-looking people. As each one stepped forward, the sultan's servant read out their crime. The sultan would consider the wrongdoing and give them a punishment.

One man had been caught stealing a donkey and was sent to the dungeons. A young woman had protected an enemy of the sultan and she was banished from the city forever.

Ali was worrying about what his punishment might be, when someone tapped him on the shoulder. It was Haroun. He leaned out of the shadows and whispered to Ali. "I saw that cook grab you, so I crept into the kitchen and borrowed this teapot. Take it, brother, I have a plan." Haroun whispered his plan into Ali's ear. It was a very cunning plan, indeed.

At last, Ali came to the front of the line. The sultan's servant pulled him forward. "This wretch was caught stealing from the palace kitchens," he said, shoving Ali in front of the sultan.

The sultan looked at Ali with fierce, dark eyes. "What do you have to say?" he said, in a deep, growling voice. Ali felt very afraid, but he remembered Haroun's plan and decided to be brave.

"I was not stealing from you, mighty sultan," he said. Ali held out the teapot. "I merely came to show you this, a prize more valuable than gold. This is an enchanted teapot and inside it, lives a genie! Behold! – I will say the secret word and the genie will appear!" Ali pretended to whisper into the teapot.

Meanwhile, Haroun had climbed up into the rafters of the hall. Just as Ali pretended to whisper, Haroun dropped a big bag of flour. It burst and sent great clouds of flour-dust into the air. Haroun jumped quietly down from the rafters and when the flour-dust cleared, everyone gasped. It was as if Haroun had appeared out of nowhere!

"I am the genie of the teapot," Haroun boomed. "What is your bidding, great master?" He bowed low to Ali.
"It's a cheap trick, my Lord," sneered the servant. "This is no genie!"
"Genie," said Ali, "I command you to show your strength. Crush one of those jewels!"

Haroun took a big ruby from a pile near the sultan and pretended to crush it. However, he secretly hid the jewel and swapped it with one of the sweets from the kitchen that he had put into his pocket. He crushed the red sweet easily, and everyone was amazed.

The servant looked shocked. "It can't be real," he said. "A real genie would be able to make treasure, not destroy it!"

Ali, turned to Haroun. "Genie, create jewels for the sultan!"
Clever Haroun had secretly taken more of the sultan's jewels and hidden them in the teapot. He picked the teapot up very slowly and stared at it. Everyone went very quiet. Haroun then shook the teapot and it rattled. When he tipped it up, gleaming jewels poured out. Everybody was fooled.

The sultan's eyes nearly popped out of his head. "I must have this enchanted teapot!" he cried. "How much does it cost?"
"It is worth more gold than your whole palace," said Ali, grandly. "But for my beloved sultan, I ask for only one jewel from your pile."
The sultan threw him a gigantic emerald and Ali gave him the teapot.

"Goodbye!" cried Haroun, still pretending to be a Genie. "I depart until the sultan calls for me." Haroun threw a large handful of flour in the air and, while no one could see him, he dashed out of the hall.

"To make the genie reappear, you have only to utter the magic word," said Ali. "Listen well, for I can say the word only once, or the magic will be destroyed!" He leaned over and whispered in the sultan's ear, "The magic word is – Habbella-babbella-zubbella-bubella-zabba-kabbo!"

With that, Ali left the hall and ran out of the palace. When he was gone, the sultan tried to summon the genie by saying Ali's made-up magic word. However, try as he might, he could not remember it.

The sultan spent so many days and nights whispering into the teapot, that eventually he forgot to sentence his people to horrible punishments. Everyone in the city was happier than they had been for years.

As for Ali and Haroun, they sold the emerald and bought a magnificent mansion. With the money left over, they were able to afford so much food that they were never hungry again.

The Ugly Duckling

Once upon a time, in the shady reeds by a river bank, a mother duck sat on top of her eggs. She had been waiting a long while for them to hatch and was getting impatient. Soon, there were cracking sounds, as little ducklings emerged from their shells. One by one, the eggs hatched, except for one. The remaining egg was much larger than the rest and its shell was grey.

Finally, the big egg cracked and a duckling emerged. It didn't look at all like the other fluffy little ducklings. It was big and clumsy and instead of being a beautiful yellow color, it was a dirty grey. It had wide feet and a long neck. Even the mother duck didn't like the look of it.

When the other birds in the farmyard saw the big duckling, they laughed and laughed. "It's the ugliest duckling we've ever seen!" they said. The mother duck and her little ducklings agreed that the strange duckling was just too ugly to have around. The hens pecked him and the turkeys chased him. No one loved the poor little ugly duckling.

One day, the ugly duckling was so fed up that he decided to leave the farmyard and find some new friends. He waddled down to the river, where some wild ducks had landed. "Perhaps they will accept me," the duckling thought and he swam over to them.

Suddenly, there was a loud cracking noise. Before the ugly duckling could speak to the ducks, they flew away in fright. Nearby, hunters fired their guns. They were looking for birds to shoot and their hunting dog was crashing through the reeds. "He'll eat me up!" thought the terrified duckling, but the dog ran right past him.

"I'm even too ugly for a dog to eat!" thought the duckling. He hid in the reeds, with his head bowed, waiting for the hunters to pass.

The ugly duckling swam down the river until it reached a little cottage near the river bank. The door of the cottage opened and a stern-faced old woman came out, followed by a red hen and a black and white cat. The woman saw the ugly duckling and grabbed hold of it. "Look, Hen. Look, Cat," she said. "Now I shall have duck eggs for my supper."

Days passed, but the duckling didn't lay any eggs. "What use are you if you can't lay eggs?" said the hen.
"Can you purr, or catch mice, or arch your back, like me?" asked the cat.
"No, I can't," admitted the little duckling.
"Then you're useless!" said the cat and the hen agreed.

The duckling was just as miserable in the cottage as he had been in the farmyard. "I don't belong here," he said, sadly. "I want to go back to the water." The hen and the cat looked at him and laughed. "What a stupid idea," said the hen, clucking her disapproval. "You really are a very silly bird," added the cat.

One day, when no one was around, the duckling waddled outside and swam off down the river again. In the distance, he saw some beautiful swans flying across the sky. The ugly duckling had never seen such magnificent birds and his heart rose at the sight of them. "I wish I could be with them," he thought sadly. "But they would never want to spend time with someone as ugly as me. I wish I were as lovely as they are."

Winter came and the weather became colder. The ugly duckling sat in the reeds, shivering and alone. The days and nights grew colder and colder until, eventually, the water froze over.

While sleeping one day, the ugly duckling was grabbed by a farmer and taken into his house. "This will make a good pet for my children," said the farmer and he put the duckling on some straw by the fire.

However, even though the farmer's house was warm and dry, the ugly duckling wasn't happy. The farmer's children teased him and chased him around the house. He flapped his wings to escape and knocked over a jug of milk, then he toppled over a basket of eggs on the table. The farmer was so cross, he blamed the little duckling and threw him out of the house.

The poor little duckling had nowhere to go, so he hid in the reeds and waited for the long, dark months of winter to pass. Snow and ice covered the land and everything was frozen.

Very slowly, winter turned into spring and the little duckling felt warm rays of sunshine on his back. The ice began to thaw and the snow began to melt. Once again, the river flowed and the duckling was able to swim. Now, however, he found that he could swim faster than before. He had grown too and his feathers had changed color.

One day, the beautiful swans flew down and landed on the river. Even though he was scared of being pecked and laughed at, the duckling decided to speak to the birds. "I don't care if they laugh at me," he thought.

The duckling swam up to the swans. "I'm just an ugly duckling," he said, sadly. "Please don't laugh at me or peck me. I only want to speak to you,"

The swans looked at each other in amazement. "Look down into the water," said one swan, softly. The ugly duckling looked down at its reflection for the first time that spring. Instead of a gawky, grey bird, it was amazed to find a beautiful white swan staring back at it.

"I'm a swan!" he cried and curved his long, slender neck in joy. The other swans were very happy to have met their new friend. "Fly with us, brother," they said and they all took off into the sky.

The ugly duckling had changed into a beautiful swan. His time of unhappiness and misfortune was over and, at last, he had found his true brothers and sisters. The swan lived a long and happy life and was never lonely again.

Hansel and Gretel

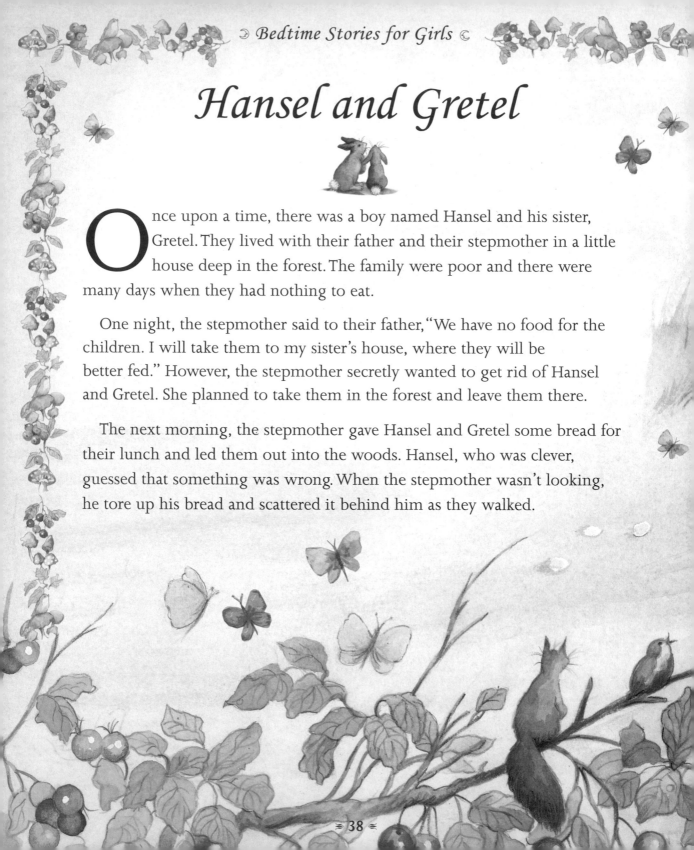

Once upon a time, there was a boy named Hansel and his sister, Gretel. They lived with their father and their stepmother in a little house deep in the forest. The family were poor and there were many days when they had nothing to eat.

One night, the stepmother said to their father, "We have no food for the children. I will take them to my sister's house, where they will be better fed." However, the stepmother secretly wanted to get rid of Hansel and Gretel. She planned to take them in the forest and leave them there.

The next morning, the stepmother gave Hansel and Gretel some bread for their lunch and led them out into the woods. Hansel, who was clever, guessed that something was wrong. When the stepmother wasn't looking, he tore up his bread and scattered it behind him as they walked.

The stepmother made Hansel and Gretel walk a very long way. When they became tired, she told them to sleep under a tree. However, while the brother and sister were sleeping, the stepmother left and returned home.

When Hansel and Gretel woke up, they found they were all alone. It was cold and dark. "Don't worry," said Hansel. "All we have to do is follow my trail of breadcrumbs back to our cottage."

But when they went to look for the trail, the children couldn't find it anywhere. The birds of the forest had eaten every single breadcrumb, so Hansel and Gretel had no way to get back home.

Hours passed and the children became more and more lost. They had wandered deep into the forest, when they saw a little house in a clearing.

The house was strange and wonderful. Hansel and Gretel had never seen anything like it. The walls were made of gingerbread, the windows were gumdrops, the door was chocolate and the chimney was a big candy cane.

The brother and sister were so hungry that they rushed up to the house and broke off a large chunk of gingerbread. They ate it ravenously and it tasted delicious.

All of a sudden, the chocolate door flew open. An ugly, old woman came rushing out. "You naughty children," she cried. "I'll teach you to eat my house." The woman grabbed Hansel and Gretel with her bony hands and dragged them inside, locking the chocolate door behind them.

The woman was a witch. She pushed Hansel into a cage that hung from the ceiling. "I'll be able to keep an eye on you up there," she said. Then, the witch made Gretel do the cleaning. "You cannot go to bed until my house is spotless," she cackled. "However, if you do a good job, you will both get lots of candy to eat."

Just as she promised, the witch gave Hansel and Gretel lots of candy to eat. At first, the children liked it, but soon they felt sick from eating sweet, sticky sugar all day and they longed for a simple piece of bread.

Each day, the witch would feel Hansel's finger through the bars of his cage and mutter to herself, "Not yet, not yet." Then, she would make Hansel eat even more sweets, but the witch never told either of the children why.

One night, Gretel heard the witch mumbling in her sleep. "Mmm, delicious! Hansel for my supper!" Gretel realized why the witch was feeding Hansel so much candy. She was fattening him up so she could eat him for her dinner!

Gretel told Hansel about the evil plan. So, the next time the witch felt Hansel's finger through the bars to see if he was fat enough to eat, Hansel stuck a twig out instead. The witch couldn't see very well, so she didn't notice. "Too skinny!" she croaked. "I won't eat you today!"

Even though the witch fed Hansel more and more candy, he always held out the twig. "Your brother is very strange," said the witch to Gretel, one day. "However much he eats, he never gets any fatter. I think I'll roast him and gobble him up as a snack!"

The witch forced Gretel to light the huge, old oven in the corner of the gingerbread house. Because Hansel wasn't fat enough for a proper supper, the witch decided to eat both children together. "Be a good girl and get in the oven and see if it's hot enough yet," said the witch, slyly. When Gretel was inside, the witch planned to close the door and roast her.

But Gretel was as clever as her brother. Instead of getting into the oven, she said, "That's funny. It doesn't seem to be warm at all." "Nonsense," said the witch. "Stand aside and let me see." And the witch climbed all the way into the hot oven.

Quick as a flash, Gretel slammed the door of the big oven and trapped the witch inside. She ran to Hansel and unlocked his cage. They were so happy to be back together again, they hugged each other as if they would never let go. "Quick!" said Gretel. "We must run!"

Before they left, Hansel went upstairs to the witch's room and searched it. Soon he found what he was looking for — a map of the forest. He ran back downstairs, flung open the chocolate door and the two children escaped.

With the help of the map, Hansel and Gretel soon found their way home. In their little house, they found their father crying. He had missed Hansel and Gretel so much. When they told him that the stepmother had abandoned them, their father sent her away forever and Hansel, Gretel and their father lived happily ever after.

The Golden Boots

A long time ago, there lived a boy prince who loved to dance. Each day, he practiced his steps with a little serving girl called Carrie. The boy prince and the serving girl became the best of friends and danced all over the palace.

One day, however, the king told his son that he could not dance with Carrie any more. "She is just a serving girl," he said, "and you are a prince. You must play with princesses."

Years passed and the prince and the serving girl grew up. The prince gave splendid balls and parties at the palace and everyone danced all night. However, the king would not allow the prince to invite Carrie. She had to work in the kitchens and serve the food at the splendid banquets.

Soon, the time came for the prince to marry. "I shall marry the girl who is the best dancer," he said. "I do not care how rich, or poor she is. Tomorrow, a banquet will be held in my honor. Afterwards, there will be a dancing competition. Whoever wins it will become my bride."

The prince secretly hoped that Carrie would enter the competition. He had not forgotten how beautifully she had danced when they were children. If she won it, his father, the king, could do nothing to stop them marrying.

Soon, the palace was full of girls practicing their dancing. Carrie watched from the shadows as they whirled and twirled in their ballgowns. "I cannot possibly hope to dance like they do," she said, sadly. "They are so elegant and beautiful."

Carrie had to clear up after the banquet. As she was walking back to the kitchen, an old lady came up to her. "I am a poor, old woman, with no food," said the old lady. "Can you spare me some bread?"

The serving girl handed the woman some food and she ate it, hungrily. "In return for your kindness," said the old woman, "I will lend you my golden boots. The person who wears them will dance better than anyone else, but you must promise to return them to me tomorrow."

Carrie thanked the old lady and promised to return the golden boots. That night, she danced with the prince, far better than any of the other girls in the palace. "This girl will be my bride!" cried the prince joyfully and they were married the very next day.

Carrie was so happy, she forgot all about the boots and her promise to the old woman. She even wore the boots under her wedding dress. She danced and danced at the wedding celebrations and was happier than she had ever been.

Hours later, Carrie was tired and wanted to sit down but found that she couldn't. The golden boots kept dancing with her in them! Carrie tried to take them off, but they wouldn't move.

Suddenly, Carrie noticed that everyone else was getting up and starting to dance, too. Solemn palace officials suddenly found themselves doing a merry jig. Grandfathers and grandmothers found that they were able to dance as well as their grandchildren. Even the members of the band were dancing as they played their instruments.

The dancing went on and on. "We can't stop," said the wedding guests in amazement. When the prince saw what was happening, he was very alarmed. Carrie told him about the old lady and the golden boots. "It must be the boots that are making everyone dance," said the prince. "We must find the old lady and return them, otherwise our guests will be exhausted."

Carrie and the prince danced out of the palace, followed by the wedding guests. They danced all the way into the town and everyone they met on the way started to dance, too.

Carrie led the people out of town and into the woods, where they saw a strange old shack. Carrie was still dancing when she knocked on the door.

The little old lady answered, "I'm so sorry that I didn't return your boots in time," said Carrie. The old lady smiled and looked at all the people who could not stop dancing.

"I should have explained that the boots are magic," she said. "They will keep on dancing until they are returned to me." Then the old lady snapped her fingers and the boots immediately stopped. Everyone stood still for a moment and then sank to the floor, exhausted.

Back at the palace, everyone agreed that, despite being so tired, it was the best party they had ever been to. "From this day onwards," said the prince, "I declare that each year, everyone will dance around the palace to celebrate the day of our marriage."

And so it was that every year, on the day that the prince and Carrie were married, everyone danced as if they wore magic golden boots.

The Weather Witch

Peter and Polly lived in a little village surrounded by bright golden cornfields. Each year, the people of the village harvested the corn and milled it in the old windmill by the brook.

One summer, no rain came and the crops stopped growing. Peter and Polly asked their father what would happen. "If it does not rain, the seeds will not grow," their father said. "There will be no harvest and we shall starve. Some might say it is time to call on the Weather Witch."

Peter and Polly wanted to know all about the Weather Witch, so their father told them. "The tale of the Weather Witch is one that is told to children when the harvest fails, so listen carefully."

"No one has ever seen the Weather Witch, but it is said that she controls the wind and the rain. She sends storms when she is angry and soft rain when she is at peace. I have heard folk say that she lives in a cave under a waterfall many days journey from here."

The very next day, Peter and Polly set out to find the Weather Witch. They were walking through a field when they saw a cat with a field mouse in its paws. "Help me!" cried the mouse, "or I'll be eaten!"

Peter scared the cat away and the mouse thanked them. "I have no gold or silver," said the mouse, "but maybe I can help you, too, one day?"

Peter and Polly journeyed further, until their small supply of food was almost gone. Deep in a forest, they came upon a pigeon. It was lying on the floor, faint with hunger. "Please, can you spare me a crumb of food?" asked the pigeon.

Polly gave the pigeon her last bite of bread. Before long, the pigeon was strong enough to fly away. "I have no gold or silver," said the pigeon, but maybe I can help you, too, one day?"

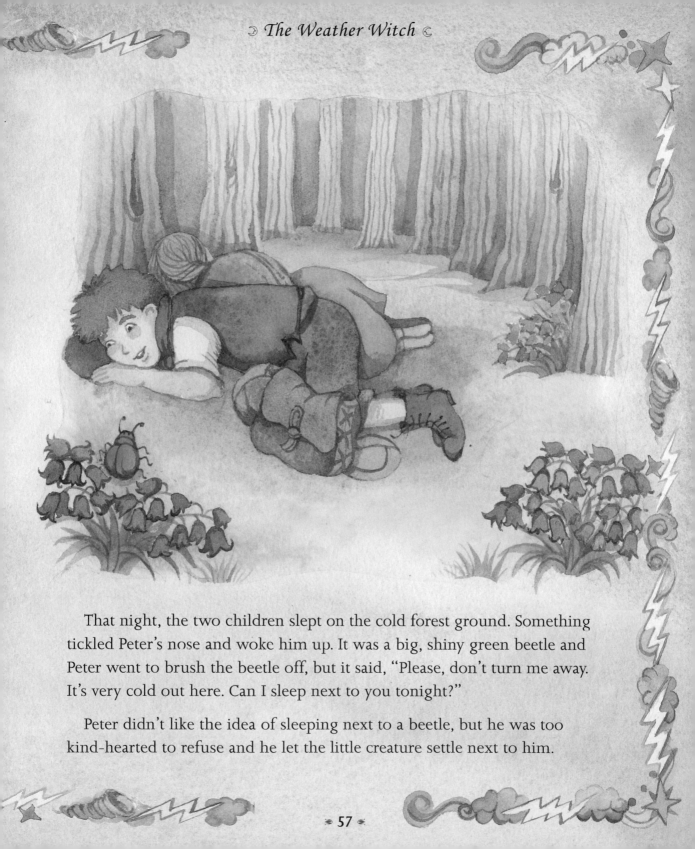

That night, the two children slept on the cold forest ground. Something tickled Peter's nose and woke him up. It was a big, shiny green beetle and Peter went to brush the beetle off, but it said, "Please, don't turn me away. It's very cold out here. Can I sleep next to you tonight?"

Peter didn't like the idea of sleeping next to a beetle, but he was too kind-hearted to refuse and he let the little creature settle next to him.

In the morning, the beetle thanked Peter and said, "I have no gold or silver, but maybe I can help you, too, one day?"

Peter and Polly continued on their way and reached a waterfall, streaming into a wild river. Behind the waterfall was a dark cave. A fierce wind blew from the cave and in the shadows, hunched and ragged, sat the Weather Witch. "What do you want?" she said, grumpily.

The children tried to hide their fear and told the witch that they needed rain for their harvest. The Weather Witch laughed and it sounded like a crack of thunder. "I will send rain to your village if you bring me three impossible things – a stone that sings, a pair of fairy's shoes and a living jewel." She cackled loudly and went into the darkness of her cave.

Peter and Polly thought about the Weather Witch's words. "What she asks is impossible," said Peter. "It's hopeless," sighed Polly. Suddenly, Peter felt something tugging at his sleeve. It was the mouse that they had rescued from the cat.

"I can help you," said the mouse. It scampered off, then returned with something in its paws. It was a stone with a hole in the middle. The children took the stone to the Weather Witch. When they held it up, the cold wind blew through it and it made a long, low whistling sound.

"A stone that sings!" said the witch. "You have done well, but what about my fairy shoes?" She sent the children back outside, where they sat wondering how they could possibly get some fairy shoes.

Just then, Polly felt something land on her shoulder. It was the pigeon they had fed earlier. "I can help you," it said. "Follow me, but be very quiet." So the children followed the pigeon to a secret grove, where they hid. Before long, when all was quiet, some fairies appeared.

The fairies danced and danced and then they fell asleep. The pigeon flew softly to them and removed a tiny pair of fairy shoes. "Don't worry, I'll return them afterwards," said the pigeon to the delighted children.

Peter and Polly rushed back to the cave and gave the fairy shoes to the Weather Witch, who scowled when she saw the second part of her task completed. "What about my living jewel?" she cried, creating an especially cold blast of wind and tossing the shoes out of the cave.

The children sat outside the cave thinking. This time, the big green beetle crawled up to them. "I would love to help you," it said, "but I have no secrets and no skill."

"Wait," said Polly. "You are the brightest green I have ever seen. You look just like a living jewel." They took the beetle into the cave, where the wind was roaring even more strongly than before. They showed the bright, shiny green beetle to the Weather Witch.

The Weather Witch took the beetle. She started to shake and make a deep, booming sound. The children got ready to run away, but then they realised that she was laughing. "You children are very clever!" chortled the Weather Witch. She handed them a glass ball. "Return to your village and break this ball."

When Peter and Polly reached their village after many days' travel, nobody believed them when they told their tale. Then the children threw the glass ball onto the ground, breaking it. Great grey clouds spilled from the broken ball, filling the sky and a gentle rain began to fall.

"It's true!" said their father, hugging them both. That year, the crops grew higher than ever. The villagers had more than enough bread to eat and Peter and Polly lived happily ever after.

The Three Little Pigs

Once upon a time, there were three little pigs who wanted to leave home. "We must build our own houses," they said. The three little pigs said goodbye to their mother and set off.

The first little pig hadn't walked very far when he met a man carrying a bale of straw. The little pig bought the bale of straw and started to build a house. When he was finished, the first little pig had a house of straw. It had a straw door, straw walls and straw windows.

The second little pig met a man carrying a great bundle of sticks. The little pig bought the sticks and made himself a house of sticks. It was stronger than the house of straw and the second little pig was very proud of it.

The third little pig walked a long way and came upon a man carrying lots of bricks. The little pig bought the bricks and built himself a house that was very strong and sturdy.

The little pigs didn't know it, but they were being watched by a hungry wolf, who loved to eat little pigs. He went to the house of straw and knocked on the door.

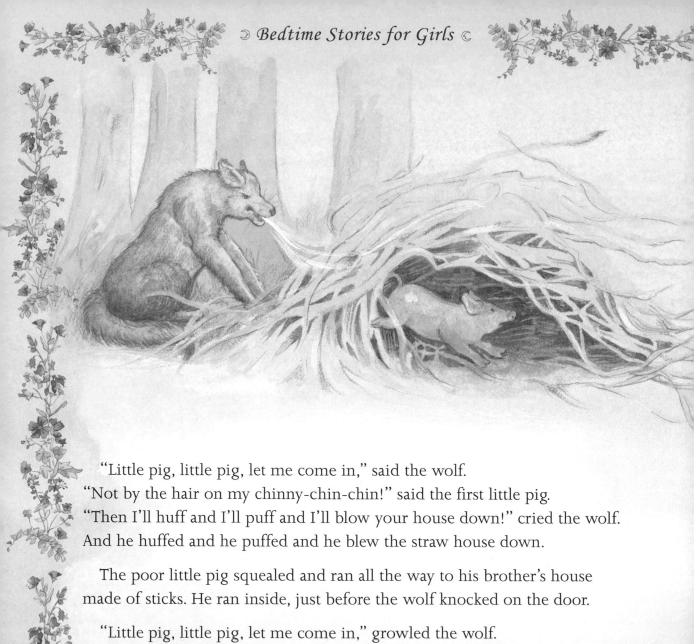

"Little pig, little pig, let me come in," said the wolf.

"Not by the hair on my chinny-chin-chin!" said the first little pig.

"Then I'll huff and I'll puff and I'll blow your house down!" cried the wolf.

And he huffed and he puffed and he blew the straw house down.

The poor little pig squealed and ran all the way to his brother's house made of sticks. He ran inside, just before the wolf knocked on the door.

"Little pig, little pig, let me come in," growled the wolf.

"Not by the hair on my chinny-chin-chin!" said the second little pig.

"Then I'll huff and I'll puff and I'll blow your house down!" said the wolf.

And he huffed and he puffed and he blew the little stick house down.

The two little pigs ran as fast as they could to the house of the third little pig. As soon as they were inside and had bolted the door, they heard a loud knocking.

"Little pig, little pig, let me come in!" said the wolf.
"Not by the hair on my chinny-chin-chin!" said the third little pig.
"Then I'll huff and I'll puff and I'll blow your house down!" said the wolf.
So he huffed and he puffed, but nothing happened!

The wolf huffed and puffed again, but still nothing happened. The third little pig's house of bricks was too sturdy and the wolf couldn't blow it down.

The wolf was out of breath, but hungrier than ever. "I'll have to trick those pigs into leaving the house," he thought. So, the wolf put on his kindest voice and tapped on the door. "You will get hungry soon, little piggies and I don't mean you any harm. Won't you come and pick some turnips with me tomorrow, at six o'clock?"

Now, the third little pig knew that the wolf wanted to eat him and his brothers, so he thought of a way to outwit him. "We'd love to pick turnips with you," he said. "Please call again tomorrow, at six o'clock."

The next day, the three little pigs tiptoed out of the house at five o'clock. They gathered all the turnips from the nearby field. Then they tiptoed back to the house. At six o'clock, the wolf knocked on the door. "Time to get turnips, little piggies!" he growled, softly.

"You're late!" shouted the third little pig. "Sorry, but we've already got the turnips!" Inside the brick house, the three little pigs were all laughing at the wolf.

The wolf was very cross, but he wasn't about to be beaten by three silly, little pigs, so he thought of another plan. "There are some juicy apples in the orchard nearby. Come with me tomorrow, at five o'clock, and I will help you pick some," he said. The little pigs agreed to meet the wolf, but first, they set about making a big pot of boiling turnip soup.
"This will come in very handy," said the third little pig.

The next day, the little pigs tiptoed out of the house at four o'clock and ran to the orchard. "We will make a fool of that silly, old wolf," they giggled, as they picked the juicy, green apples.

But the wily wolf had guessed what the pigs were up to and he went to the orchard early, too. He found the three little pigs with a big basket of apples, all ready to go home. He growled and chased them out of the orchard, all the way back to the brick house, but the pigs got inside just in time.

Now the wolf was really angry. He snarled and jumped onto the roof of the little brick house. "Little pigs," he growled, "I'm going to eat you all up!" Then he jumped down the chimney.

What the wolf didn't know was that at the bottom of the chimney was the pot of turnip soup. He fell into it with a great big SPLASH and got such a fright, he ran away and never bothered the little pigs ever again.

The three little pigs were very happy to be free of the big, bad, wolf. The third little pig built his two brothers brand new houses made of bricks, just like his own and they all lived safely and happily ever after.

The Mouse and the Dragon

Once upon a time, in a wild meadow, there was a little field mouse who wanted to be noticed. "I'm so small that no one ever seems to pay me any attention," he said.

One day, when the field mouse was dozing outside his little nest, he saw a big dragonfly. It flapped its wings and buzzed round and round the sleepy mouse. "Shoo!" cried the field mouse. He picked up a blade of grass and waved it at the dragonfly, which flew off immediately.

The mouse was very pleased with himself. He decided to tell all his friends how brave he was. He went to find his friend, the vole. "I am the bravest mouse that ever lived!" he said. "For I defeated a dragonfly with a only blade of grass!"

The vole was a little hard of hearing. "What's that?" he mumbled. "You defeated a dragon?" The field mouse had already scampered off. So, the vole went and told his friend, the shrew. "Did you hear what happened? The field mouse defeated a dragon with a blade of grass!"

As it happened, the shrew was also rather deaf. She went and told her friend the hedgehog. "You must hear the latest news," she said. "The field mouse defeated a dragon with a mighty blade!"

So the hedgehog went to visit the field mouse. "What an amazing mouse you are," she said. "To defeat a dragon with a mighty sword is a very brave thing to do indeed."

The field mouse was so happy to be noticed, he didn't tell the hedgehog what had really happened. Instead, he just nodded his head and agreed. "Yes, I am rather brave, aren't I?" he said.

Soon, all the animals believed that the field mouse had defeated a dragon. Everywhere the field mouse went, he was treated like a hero. He was given all kinds of presents and everyone invited him round to dinner, until his tummy was filled to bursting.

The news of the field mouse's adventure spread far and wide, over the hedges and fields, through the forest, all the way to the faraway mountains, where a real dragon lived.

The dragon was amazed at the story of the field mouse. He decided to fly down from the mountains and see what all the fuss was about. So he spread his great wings and flew all the way to the meadow, where the little field mouse lived.

The vole, the shrew and the hedgehog saw the huge dragon land in the middle of the meadow. "Come quick!" they all shouted to the field mouse. "There is a dragon in the meadow. You must defeat him!"

The field mouse climbed to the top of a bush to have a look. When he saw the dragon, the field mouse almost dropped off the bush in fright. "I'll stay very quiet," he thought, "and perhaps the dragon will go away."

The dragon examined its sharp claws and called out, "Excuse me, I have heard that a mighty dragon-slayer lives here. I have come to fight him and if I win, this meadow will be mine."

A young rabbit spotted the field mouse on the bush. "Look over there, Mister Dragon," the rabbit called out. "There's the dragon-slayer." The rabbit pointed to the field mouse, who was pretending to be invisible.

When the dragon saw the field mouse, he started to laugh. When a dragon laughs, he blows flame everywhere. Several trees nearly caught on fire and the field mouse coughed from all the smoke. When the dragon finally finished laughing, he wiped his eyes. "I'm terribly sorry," he boomed. "I've never seen such a small dragon-slayer in all my five hundred years! Brave Sir Mouse, come out and fight me and we will see which of us is the strongest!"

The field mouse thought quickly. "Instead of a fight," he said, in his squeaky little voice, "let us have a competition. In the field across the way lives a farmer and his wife. Whoever can make them come outside will be the winner."

The dragon thought this sounded like a very easy task. "I shall go first," he said and he stomped across to the farmhouse to look in the window. The dragon roared and stamped his feet. He flapped his wings and blew huge jets of flame into the air.

However, instead of running out of the house, the farmer and his wife ran upstairs and hid under the bed. No matter how much noise and flame the dragon made, the farmer and his wife wouldn't come out of the house. They were too afraid of being eaten.

Finally, the dragon gave up. He stomped back to the meadow in a very bad mood. "Your turn, little mouse," he roared, grumpily.

The field mouse scampered across the fields to the farmhouse and crawled under the gap in the front door. He ran all the way up to the bedroom, scurried under the bed and squeaked at the farmer and his wife.

The farmer's wife looked horrified. "It's a mouse!" she screamed and ran downstairs with the field mouse scurrying after her. She was so scared, the poor woman opened the front door and ran outside, still screaming.

"Come back!" yelled the farmer. "There's a dragon outside." But his wife kept on running. So the farmer ran after her to make sure she didn't get eaten by the dragon.

The field mouse returned to the hedge. "I'm amazed," said the dragon. "You really must be a mighty warrior. I'm glad I didn't fight you." With that, the dragon said goodbye and flew back up to the mountains, never to return.

Now the field mouse really was a hero. The vole, the shrew and the hedgehog held a special party for him and this time, he really deserved it!

The Witch's Well

Once upon a time, there was a princess who lived in a land where everything was so dry that hardly any food could grow. One day, the king said to the princess, "We don't have enough food in the palace for you to eat. You must leave us now, to seek your fortune. Maybe you can find a way to bring water back to the land?"

The princess left the palace with only a crust of bread to eat. She walked for miles, through withered forests and dried-up fields. Eventually, she came to a dark and dusty castle. "Perhaps the people in the castle will give me some food," she thought. So the princess knocked on the door.

The door was opened by an old woman, wearing a blue dress and a pointed hat. "Come in, my dear," she said. As soon as the princess stepped into the castle, the huge door slammed shut behind her. "You are my prisoner now," said the old woman, who was really a wicked witch. "You must work for me."

The princess was forced to sweep the floors of the castle and bring the witch all the horrible ingredients to put into her cauldron. From dawn until dusk, the princess slaved for the witch and at night, she was forced to sleep on a bed of straw in the cold courtyard. No matter how hard she dusted and swept, nothing in the castle ever seemed to get clean.

In the middle of the courtyard was an old well. The witch had forbidden the princess to go anywhere near it. However, one night, she heard a small voice that seemed to come from inside. "Help me!" it called. So the princess crept quietly over to have a look.

"Please, help me," called the small voice, again. It was coming from the bottom of the well. The princess could not see who the voice belonged to, so she lowered herself down in the old bucket that was used to draw water from the well. Down and down went the bucket, until it was far from the surface.

The well was so deep, the princess could hardly see the opening above her. At the bottom, there was nothing, except a little toad. "Please, help me!" said the toad. "I am a prince who has been enchanted by the witch and trapped down here. The only way I can escape is by swimming up through water, but the witch has drained the well of water."

"I am trapped in the castle," said the princess. "I cannot free you."
"There is a way," said the toad. "The witch cast a spell to suck the water from this well and all the land around into a magic bottle. She keeps the bottle by her bed and if you can get it, we can use it to free ourselves and restore the land to life again."

"I will try to get the bottle," said the princess and she pulled herself up out of the well. She crept silently across the courtyard, so as not to wake the witch. Then the princess curled up on her straw bed and thought about how to get the bottle that held all the water of the land.

Every day, the princess tried to find a way to sneak into the witch's room in the tallest tower. But the witch kept the room locked and the only time it was open was when the witch was asleep.

One night, the princess climbed to the top of the tower and crept into the witch's room. The witch was fast asleep and snoring. The princess opened a wooden chest near the bed. She took out the magic bottle and put it in her pocket. However, as the princess opened the door to leave, it creaked loudly.

Suddenly, the witch sat up in bed. "How dare you enter my room!" she screeched. The witch jumped up, grabbed the princess and pulled her downstairs and across the courtyard to the well.

The witch made the princess climb into the bucket, then she lowered it to the bottom of the well and cut the rope. "Now you're trapped, forever," shrieked the witch. "You can stay down there with that slimy toad."

The princess began to cry. "We'll never escape now," she sobbed.
"Don't worry," said the toad. "I have a plan. Did you get the bottle?"
"Yes, said the princess. "I put it in my pocket before the witch woke up."
"Uncork it," said the toad, "and be ready to swim!"

The princess pulled the cork out of the bottle. Suddenly, all the water of
the land gushed out. It soon filled up the old well and the princess and the
toad floated to the surface. The water carried on flowing. It filled the
courtyard of the castle and spilled over the turrets, flooding the dusty, dry
land all around.

The witch heard the noise and opened her chest to find that the magic bottle was gone. She ran down from her tower in a rage, but a great wave carried her out of the castle far, far away and she was never seen again.

The waters seeped into the baked ground and the earth was no longer parched. Soon, everything began to grow and the land was green and fertile once more.

The curse on the toad was lifted and he became a noble prince once again. When the princess saw him, she fell in love with him.

The prince and the princess returned to the princess' palace, where her parents greeted her with joy. The prince and the princess were soon married and lived happily ever after.

The Farm Girl and Her Dog

Once upon a time, there was an orphan girl who lived on a farm. She worked very hard, tending the crops, feeding the chickens and herding the sheep, with the help of a faithful, old sheepdog.

One day, however, the farmer told the girl that he had sold the farm. The new owners had their own workers and did not need the girl. So the lonely orphan had to leave with no money, no friends and nowhere to go.

The girl travelled to the nearest village and looked for work, but there was none to be had. She even tried to beg for a crust of bread, but everyone ignored her. In despair, the poor girl sat by the side of the road and cried. It seemed that nobody would help her.

Suddenly, the girl felt a wet nose nuzzle her. It was the old sheepdog from the farm. The girl was overjoyed to see him. "Don't cry, mistress," said the dog. "I can help you."

The farm girl was amazed that the dog could talk. She had worked with him all those years and he had never said a word.

The dog explained to the girl how he could help. "Far away from here," he said, "there is a grand palace, with warm beds and all the food you can eat. If you will come with me, I will show you the way."

The farm girl thought for a while. She was already tired and cold, but she had nowhere to go and no one to take care of her, so she agreed to follow the dog to the palace.

The dog and the girl walked out of the town and up into the hills. Far, far away, she could see a grand building on a steep hill. "That is the palace," said the dog. "It is many days away."

That night, the farm girl and the dog slept in a rocky hollow. The farm girl shivered with the cold, so the dog lay next to her to keep her warm. When daylight came, the dog guided the farm girl across an open meadow. A storm began to gather overhead and they ran into a nearby forest. The forest was dim and cold, but at least it was dry.

All day long, the farm girl and her dog walked through the gloomy forest. As dusk fell, the girl could see many pairs of yellow eyes peering through the trees. She began to feel afraid and walked close by the dog's side. Before long, they were surrounded by vicious, grey wolves.

Suddenly, to the girl's surprise, the dog began to grow larger. It turned into a shaggy, golden wolf. Whenever the grey wolves came close, it snapped and snarled to keep them away and protect the girl. Eventually, the grey wolves gave up and left. When they had gone, the golden wolf turned back into a dog again.

The next day, the farm girl and her dog came to a bridge across a shimmering waterfall. The farm girl was about to cross the bridge, but the dog told her to stay back. "I smell danger," the dog said.

Just as the dog stepped onto the bridge, a huge black bear came bounding across from the other side. Its teeth were sharp and its claws were as long as knives. It growled and launched at the dog.

Suddenly, the dog grew and grew until it was a great, golden bear. The two bears met in the middle of the bridge and fought savagely. Eventually, the golden bear threw the evil black bear down into the water below. Then the golden bear changed back into a dog.

The dog led the girl safely across the bridge and they walked on until they came to the foot of a steep hill. On top of the hill was the shining palace. However, between them and the palace stood a vast maze.

Together, the dog and the farm girl entered the maze. They wandered for a long time, down many dead ends, before they finally got to the centre. There, a huge, brown lion stood guard. It gave a menacing roar when it saw them.

The dog began to grow again and this time, he turned into a golden lion. The two lions fought with all their might. The brown lion was strong and bold and he yowled and snarled and scratched the golden lion.

Soon, the golden lion was knocked to the floor. The farm girl watched in horror, as the brown lion leaned over him and was about to give him a deadly bite with his razor sharp teeth.

The farm girl was afraid, but she had to save her friend, so she ran up to the brown lion. The girl grabbed his tail and yanked it as hard as she possibly could. The brown lion roared with pain and the golden lion jumped out from under its grasp, then growled with such ferocity that the brown lion ran away.

Immediately, the golden lion turned back into a dog. He sniffed around the centre of the maze and found a secret passageway. "Walk through this tunnel," said the dog. "I will follow you."

So the farm girl walked through the dark tunnel. At the end of it, she found herself in the beautiful garden of the palace. When she looked around to tell her faithful, old sheepdog, she found that he had turned into a handsome prince in elegant robes.

The prince took her hand. "This is my palace," he said. "I was cursed by my own selfishness and greed to be a humble dog, until I could truly help someone without asking for anything in return."

The farm girl took one look at the prince and fell in love. "You have saved my life many times over," she said. "How can I thank you?"

"Be my bride," said the prince and the farm girl gratefully agreed. They were soon married and they lived in safety and happiness in the palace for the rest of their lives.

The Magic Cake

Once there was a young princess who was greatly loved by all the servants in her palace. Although she was happy to spend time with her royal parents, the princess enjoyed sneaking away to visit the palace kitchens.

The chief cook was the princess' special friend. She was a big, round woman with twinkling eyes. Her hands were dusty with flour and her cheeks were always rosy-red. The cook was cheerful most of the time, except when the greedy palace cats tried to steal food from her kitchen table. Then the cook would wave her rolling pin and chase them away.

Each day, the princess helped the cook make pies and pastries and sometimes she was allowed to lick the sticky spoon when the cook was making her famous cakes.

The princess' birthday was approaching, so she decided to invite all her friends to a big party to celebrate. It was going to be the social event of the season and the princess couldn't wait to eat her birthday cake.

One night, just before her birthday, the princess ran down the stairs to the big kitchen, but when she opened the door, the princess got a surprise. The cook was waving her rolling pin like a magic wand. Around her, all the pots, pans and cutlery were jumping into the kitchen sink to clean themselves. Then they dried themselves and flew into the kitchen cupboards.

When the cook saw the princess, she made all the magic disappear with a wave of her rolling-pin wand. "I'm an enchantress," explained the cook, "but if people saw me use my powers, they might think I was a witch, so I only use them to clean the kitchen. If you agree to keep my secret, I will make you an extra-special birthday cake."

The princess agreed to keep the cook's secret. She would never have told on her friend, anyway. Still, she was very excited that she was going to get a special birthday cake.

The princess told all her friends about the extra-special cake, but when her birthday arrived and all the guests went to sit at the table, the princess was disappointed to see a simple cake with nothing more than white icing and a few candles in the middle.

"How dull!" said some of the guests to each other and laughed. The princess wished she hadn't said anything to her friends. She cut the cake anyway and gave a slice to each of the guests.

As the princess was cutting a piece of cake for herself, she noticed a slip of paper stuck to the icing. It had a message from the cook which said, "More cake changes you back." The princess was very puzzled, but she took a big bite of the delicious cake and thought about what the note might mean.

Suddenly, the princess felt a tickle on her shoulders. Looking round, she saw that she had sprouted bright, feathery rainbow wings. When she looked around the table, she saw that all her guests were growing wings, too.

Next, the party guests began to shrink and became the size of fairies. Everyone squealed with excitement as they realised they could fly.

"I knew the cake would be magic!" said the princess and she led her guests out into the palace corridors. They giggled and shrieked with delight, as they flew into every room, swooping and diving. They were like excited fairies, flitting here, there and everywhere.

After lots of zooming around the huge palace, the party guests began to feel tired. Flying was fun, but it was very hard work. "We can't keep our wings, forever," they said. "But how do we change back?"

The princess remembered the note from the cook. Now she understood what it meant. "We have to eat more cake," said the princess.

So, with a great fluttering of their rainbow wings, everyone flew back to the cake on the table. But the greedy palace cats had got there first. They were eating the cake and hissed at anyone who tried to stop them.

"If we don't eat more cake," said the princess, "we'll have to stay this size forever!" The princess swooped down towards the table. The cats swiped at her with their sharp claws, but she was too fast for them and grabbed a huge piece of cake.

As soon as the princess and the guests had eaten the cake, they lost their wings and grew to their full size again. Everyone was exhausted, but happy. "That was the best party ever!" said the guests.

The princess thanked the cook for her special cake. The cook promised that, at least once a year, on her birthday, the princess would always have some magic cake, so that she and her friends could fly like real fairies.

The Emperor's New Clothes

A long time ago, there lived an emperor who loved clothes more than anything else. Instead of trying to care for his people, he spent all the kingdom's money on fine, new garments. There was nothing the emperor liked more than parading his new clothes in front of everyone, so they could say how elegant he looked.

One day, two cunning thieves arrived at the emperor's palace. "This silly emperor loves clothes so much," they agreed, "it will be easy to make him shower us with gold." So the thieves went to the emperor and introduced themselves. "We are the finest tailors in the world," they said. "We will make you the best suit of clothes that there has ever been."

At first, the emperor didn't believe them. "I have seen all the finest clothes the world has to offer," he said. "What can you two do that is better than what I have seen already?"

"We have a roll of magic cloth," they said. "It has the finest colors and patterns you have ever seen. It is so exquisite that only the cleverest, most refined people can see it. It is invisible to anyone who is incredibly stupid, or who does not deserve to be doing his job."

"That sounds marvellous," said the emperor, clapping his hands. "If I have a suit of this material, I will know exactly which of my ministers deserves his job and I can make sure I am not surrounded by stupid people."

The thieves looked at each other and smiled. "The magic material is very expensive to make," said one thief. "I'm not sure your excellency can afford it," said the other.

"Nonsense!" shouted the emperor. "Here, take a thousand gold coins, that should be more than enough to make the suit."

The thieves left the palace with the money and used it to buy two huge looms for weaving cloth. But, because they had made up the story of the cloth, there was nothing to weave.

For weeks and weeks, the swindlers spent their money on whatever they liked and did no work at all. Then, one day, there was a knock on their door. It was the emperor and all his men. "We have come to see how my suit is progressing," said the emperor.

The two thieves turned the handles of the looms with nothing on them, and cut through the air with scissors. "See, Your Excellency," they said. "Isn't it the most marvellous cloth you have ever seen?"

The emperor was shocked. He couldn't see any cloth at all. "Oh, no!" he thought. "It's just as I always thought. I'm either too stupid to see the cloth, or I don't deserve to be emperor. Nobody must ever know, or they would never let me rule." So he said to the thieves, "Yes, of course, it's certainly the finest cloth I have ever seen."

The thieves showed the imaginary cloth to the emperor's court, too. Each of them thought the same thing, "I must be too stupid or unworthy to see the cloth. I will pretend I can see it, so that the emperor does not punish me."

All the emperor's men pointed and applauded and said how fine the cloth was. "Of course, we'll need another thousand gold coins to finish it off," said the thieves. "After all, you wouldn't want to go outside with it half-finished like this." So, the emperor gave them the money without delay.

Many more weeks passed and the thieves returned to the palace. "We have finished the suit of clothes for you, Your Excellency," they said. They took the emperor into his room and pretended to fit the clothes on top of his under garments. "The cloth is so very fine and light, that only those with the most delicate skin can feel it," the thieves said. The emperor couldn't feel anything, of course, but he didn't want to look coarse and rough. "Oh, yes," he said. "It feels lighter than air."

When they were done, the thieves stood back and looked at the emperor, who was wearing nothing at all. "Our finest work!" the thieves said. "You are a marvel of modern fashion."

The emperor summoned his courtiers and they walked through the streets of the city. Everyone had heard of the magic cloth. To make sure nobody thought they were stupid, they all pretended that they could see the emperor's new clothes.

The procession wound its way through every street, even the very poorest ones. As they were passing one tiny house, a little girl and her father came out to watch them go past. The child hadn't heard about the magic cloth. "Look, Daddy," she said, "that funny man has come out in his underwear."

The child's father saw that his daughter was right. "You speak the truth, my dear," he said, laughing. "The emperor has no new clothes!"

The family next door heard the man and knew that what he said was true. "The emperor has no new clothes," they shouted. The message passed quickly from door to door and from street to street, until everyone in the city was pointing and laughing at the emperor. "The emperor has no new clothes!" they cried.

Finally, the emperor understood that what everyone was saying was true. At first, he was so embarrassed, he couldn't speak, but then he too began to laugh, until he thought his sides would split. "I have been a proud and foolish man," he said to everyone, "and I have learned my lesson."

The thieves had fled the city and were never seen there again, but the emperor became a good and wise ruler who cared more about his people than his pride and so the emperor and his people lived happily ever after.

The China Pony

Once upon a time, there was a girl named Snowdrop who lived with her father in a tiny, tumbledown cottage on the side of a high mountain. One day, a strange old woman arrived at their cottage. "I am your long-lost aunt," she said. "I have travelled a great distance to come and take care of you."

But the aunt was nasty. When Snowdrop's father wasn't looking, she would scold and snap at Snowdrop and make her scrub the floors, wash the dishes and clean all the clothes.

One morning, Snowdrop woke to find her aunt standing over her. "Your father has had to go away," said the aunt, sternly. "Now get up, you lazy girl. There are chores to be done."

From then on, Snowdrop was always unhappy. Her aunt made her go to the nearby village and buy all the best food, but when she returned, her aunt would eat it all and only toss Snowdrop a crust of bread. She even made Snowdrop sleep outside in the freezing cold. Snowdrop often thought of running away. "What if my father comes back and I'm gone?" she would think. "It would break his heart."

One day, when she was buying food in the village shop, Snowdrop saw a small, white china pony on the shelf. "How much is the pony?" she asked the shopkeeper, but he didn't know.
"I've never seen it before," the shopkeeper said. "Please, take it. Maybe it was meant for you."

Snowdrop took the china pony home. She was afraid that if her aunt saw the pony, she would take it away. So Snowdrop hid it under her pillow.

In the middle of the night, Snowdrop woke up to find something nuzzling her face. It was a beautiful, white pony "I am the china pony," it said. "Come, sit on my back."

Snowdrop climbed onto the pony's back. Suddenly, they were outside. "I am here to help you rescue your father," said the pony. "The old woman is not really your aunt at all. She is an evil sorceress and she has imprisoned him in a castle, guarded by an ogre."

"The castle is many days' travel from here, on a tower of rock that cannot be climbed," said the pony, "and when the sun rises today, the ogre will eat your father."

Snowdrop wept. "Oh, china pony, is there nothing you can do?" "There may be one thing," replied the pony. "On the mountain, a single golden flower grows. It is said to grant the power of flight. We could use this flower to help your father escape. However, nobody has ever found it."

Snowdrop and the pony spent all night on the cold mountainside, looking for the golden flower, but they found nothing. Exhausted, Snowdrop lay down in the snow. The dawn was breaking and as the first rays of the sun hit the mountainside, Snowdrop saw a golden glow in the snow. It was the golden flower!

"We do not have much time," said the pony. "When the sun is up, the ogre will eat your father." Snowdrop picked the flower and the pony ate it. Snowdrop got on the pony's back and it leaped from the mountain top, but it didn't fall. Instead, it flew through the sky.

Snowdrop and the china pony flew through the air and landed at the bottom of the castle, just before the sun was in the sky. "The ogre's tower has three levels," said the pony. "On each level, there is a chest full of treasure. Do not touch it, but go straight past."

So Snowdrop entered the castle. On the first level, there was a chest full of gold coins, but Snowdrop passed it by. On the second level, there was a chest twice as big, filled with diamonds, rubies and emeralds, but Snowdrop didn't touch any of them.

Snowdrop ran up the stairs to the third level of the castle. An enormous chest lay in the middle of the room, filled to the brim with gold, beautiful jewellery and sparkling stones.

Behind the chest, an ugly, green ogre was snoring loudly. In the corner of the tower, chained to the wall, was Snowdrop's father.

Snowdrop tiptoed up to the ogre. She saw a large key tucked into his belt. Carefully, she slid the key out of the belt and unlocked the chains. Snowdrop's father was overjoyed to see her.

As they made their way silently toward the staircase, Snowdrop's foot touched a jewel that had fallen out of the treasure chest. Suddenly, the chest slammed shut and the ogre awoke. It looked around, bleary-eyed and said in a thunderous voice, "Who is stealing my treasure?" The ogre saw Snowdrop and her father disappearing down the staircase. It let out a terrible roar and thundered after them.

Snowdrop and her father ran downstairs as quickly as they could. Behind them, they could hear the fierce ogre thudding down the steps with his great, clumsy feet.

Outside, Snowdrop pushed her father onto the pony and she jumped on behind him. The ogre had almost reached them when the white pony lifted off into the air and flew far away from the ogre and the castle.

However, Snowdrop's aunt, the wicked sorceress, sent thunder and lightning to knock them from the sky, but the white pony was too fast. He avoided every blast and kicked the lightning with his hooves, sending it crashing back to hit the sorceress, who disappeared in shower of sparks.

The white pony landed safely outside the tiny, tumbledown cottage. Snowdrop and her father climbed down and hugged one another. They turned to thank the china pony, but it was gone. In its place was a handsome prince.

"I was enchanted by the sorceress," he explained. "She turned me into a china ornament by day and a white pony by night. Now she is dead, the enchantment is lifted and I can ask for Snowdrop's hand in marriage." It wasn't long before the prince and Snowdrop were married and they were never bothered by the wicked enchantress again.

The Bee and the Butterfly

O nce, there was a furry, little caterpillar who lived on a branch of an old oak tree. The caterpillar was best friends with a busy bee who lived in a hive inside the oak.

One day, the little caterpillar said to the bee, "It is time for me to go into my cocoon and become a butterfly. We must say goodbye."
"Don't forget about me," said the busy bee, but the caterpillar had already crawled into her little cocoon and was fast sleep.

The bee busied himself collecting nectar from the nearby flowers and bringing it back to the hive to make honey. Sometimes, he would think of his old friend and wonder when he would see her again.

One day, the cocoon suddenly broke open and a shimmering butterfly emerged. When the bee saw the butterfly, he waved to her. "It's me," he said. "Your best friend, the bee!"

The butterfly had spent so long in the cocoon and had changed so much that she had forgotten her old friend. "I'm sorry," said the butterfly, "but I'm sure someone as beautiful as I am wouldn't be friends with such a small creature as you."

The busy bee was very hurt by what the butterfly had said. He flew straight back to his hive, crying all the way. "Never mind," said the other bees, "you can come and collect nectar with us." That is just what the busy little bee did. Soon, he felt much better.

All that summer, the butterfly spent her days fluttering and lazing around. When she was hungry, she just fluttered from flower to flower. She landed on the delicate petals and drank as much sweet nectar as she liked.

The bees worked hard, gathering more and more nectar for honey. "What a waste of time," the butterfly thought, sipping nectar.

As the days began to get colder, the bee approached the butterfly again. "Please be careful," said the bee. "Soon, the flowers will wither and die and there will be no more nectar."

The butterfly giggled and flew away from the bee. "Go away, little bee," she said. "I'm sure the flowers will last forever."

One night, there was a terrible storm. The wind howled and whistled. The butterfly was nearly blown away and had to hide in a hollow of an old tree trunk. Outside, the wind blew every single flower away.

The butterfly searched all around, but couldn't find any food. She was about to set off to look for more flowers somewhere else, when she saw the bee. "Don't worry," said the bee. "We have plenty of honey in the hive. Please, join us."

However, the butterfly was too proud to enter the hive. Instead, she fluttered as far away as she could in search of more flowers.

The butterfly flew and flew, but could only spot a few tiny flowers with hardly any nectar inside them. She travelled for days and days, while the air got colder and the leaves began to float down from the trees.

One evening, the butterfly could find no flowers at all. However hard she looked, she couldn't find a single one. "This can't be right," thought the butterfly in fear. Being so young, she didn't know that almost all flowers die in the winter.

That night, the butterfly was cold and hungry. When she finally got to sleep, she had a very strange dream. She dreamt that she didn't have any wings and her legs were short and stubby. Instead of being brightly colored, she was a dull green. The butterfly wasn't drinking sweet nectar, she was munching on a big leaf. In the dream, someone was with her. It was the bee.

The butterfly woke up. Now she remembered what had happened. "I was a caterpillar," she said aloud. "I was small once, just like the bee. How silly of me to forget!" Then the butterfly thought of everything she had done. "My poor friend, the bee," she cried. "What must he think of me."

The butterfly flew all the way back towards the old oak tree, even though she was so hungry, she could barely move. Finally, the butterfly saw the old oak tree. With a last effort, she landed on the hive.

"Please tell the bee I am sorry," she gasped. "How can he ever forgive me?" Some of the other bees heard her and called to the bee. He was so happy to see the butterfly, he buzzed for joy. "I'm so glad you're back," he said. "I was very worried about you."
The bee took the butterfly into the hive, where it was warm and cosy.

The butterfly looked around. Huge stacks of honeycomb reached up as far as she could see. Every bee inside the hive was full and warm.
"I wish I had saved up some nectar," she said. "You were right to work, instead of play all day."

"Don't worry," said the bee, kindly. "We have more honey than we can eat. You are welcome to stay and have as much honey as you want."

So the butterfly stayed in the beehive all winter. She had learned a great lesson from her bee friends and did her best to be especially kind and polite to them. She even helped the bees with all the work of the hive.

In time, the short winter days grew longer. Spring arrived once more and the flowers came back in bloom. Once again, the bees started to fly around the beautiful flower heads and bring in nectar for the honey. This time, however, they had an extra helper. She was a shimmering, happy and very gracious butterfly.

Little Red Riding Hood

Once upon a time, a little girl lived in a cottage with her mother, near the edge of a big, dark wood. She had a lovely, bright red cape with a hood and the little girl wore it so often, everyone called her Little Red Riding Hood.

One day, news reached the cottage that Little Red Riding Hood's grandmother was ill. So, her mother gave her a basket of delicious cakes to take to Granny. "Now, listen carefully," said Little Red Riding Hood's mother. "Remember to stay on the path that goes through the woods. You must not stop to pick flowers and don't talk to any strangers on the way."

The woods were deep and dark, even in the middle of the day, but Little Red Riding Hood wasn't scared. Even though she could see the beautiful flowers that grew along the side of the path, she obeyed her mother and did not stop to pick any of them. What Little Red Riding Hood did not know was that, deep in the shadowy trees, a wolf was watching her.

The wolf slunk out of the trees, swishing its bushy tail. "Who are you and where are you going, little girl?" he said.

Little Red Riding Hood had never seen a wolf before, so she wasn't scared. She forgot what her mother had told her about talking to strangers. "My name is Little Red Riding Hood," she said. "I'm off to visit my grandmother who lives on the other side of the wood."

"Really? How very interesting," said the wolf. "You should pick your grandmother some pretty flowers." "But my mother told me to stay on the path," said Little Red Riding Hood.

"It's very rude to go visiting someone without any flowers," said the wolf. "Anyway, I must be going now, goodbye." With that the wolf slunk off, back into the forest, as if he had never been there at all.

"How strange," thought Little Red Riding Hood. She continued on her way, but she couldn't help thinking about what the wolf had said. "Maybe Granny would like some flowers," she thought.

Further along the path, Little Red Riding Hood noticed some particularly pretty blooms. She couldn't resist any longer and left the path to pick some to give to her grandmother.

There were so many beautiful flowers to choose from, Little Red Riding Hood didn't realize how much time it was taking her. A long time passed before she had collected a perfect bouquet

"Hello," said a voice. It made Little Red Riding Hood jump. She turned to see a woodcutter, who was carrying an axe. "It's getting late," said the woodcutter. "You shouldn't be on your own in the wood."

Little Red Riding Hood told the woodcutter all about her journey. "Best be on your way then," he said, kindly. "Your grandmother will be waiting for you."

Meanwhile, the wolf had ran all the way to Little Red Riding Hood's grandmother's house. He knocked on the door and spoke with a high, girlish voice. "Hello, Granny, it's Little Red Riding Hood, can I come in?"

Grandmother got out of bed, hobbled to the door and unlocked it. The nasty wolf grabbed hold of poor Granny, tied a handkerchief round her mouth and pushed her into a cupboard. Then, the cunning wolf put on some of Granny's clothes and got into bed.

A while later, Little Red Riding Hood finally reached her grandmother's house. She knocked on the door. "Hello, Granny, it's Little Red Riding Hood, can I come in?"
"Yes, of course, my child," said the wolf, in his best grandmother's voice.

Little Red Riding Hood came in and went over to the bed. "You must excuse my voice," said the wolf, with the sheets drawn right up to his chin. "I've been so ill, it's made me quite hoarse. Come over here and sit on the bed, my dear."

Little Red Riding Hood sat on the bed and looked at the wolf.
"Oh, Granny, what big ears you have," she said.
"All the better to hear you with," said the wolf.

Little Red Riding Hood leaned in a little bit closer. "Oh, Granny, what big eyes you have."

"All the better to see you with," said the wolf.

Little Red Riding Hood began to feel there was something wrong. She looked at the wolf's paws holding the sheet. "Oh, Granny, what big hands you have."

"All the better to hug you with," said the wolf.

Little Red Riding Hood leaned in closer still, to get a better look. "Oh, Granny, what big teeth you have."

"All the better to EAT you with!" cried the wolf, as he sprang out of the bed

But Little Red Riding Hood was a lot faster than her poor grandmother and she jumped out of the way just in time. The wolf chased her round and round the bed. Suddenly, there was a knock at the door. Little Red Riding Hood ran over and flung the door open. Outside, stood the woodcutter.

The woodcutter had decided to check on Little Red Riding Hood and her grandmother to make sure that they were safe. The moment he saw the wolf, the woodcutter swung his axe and chased the nasty creature out of the house and into the dark wood. The wolf got such a fright, he ran away and never came back again.

Little Red Riding Hood let her poor old granny out of the cupboard. She made a drink and Granny, the woodcutter and Little Red Riding Hood ate some of the delicious cakes from the basket. After that, Little Red Riding Hood promised never to stray from the path, ever again.

The Tin Whistle

Once upon a time, there was a princess who lived in an old, grey castle. Everyone who lived in the castle was sad. Even the king and queen were gloomy.

The castle was filled with dusty old furniture, suits of armour and paintings of unhappy-looking ancestors. The princess found it quite funny, in fact, that she was the only cheerful one in the castle. However, try as she might, the princess could never raise anyone's spirits.

Sometimes, the princess would go for a walk in her favourite part of the garden. There, in a quiet corner, was a statue of a handsome young man, dressed as a prince. The young man's face had a very sad expression and the princess often wondered what had made him so unhappy.

One day, the princess was playing near the statue when she saw something shining in its stone hand. She climbed up and found a small, golden key. "I'm sure this wasn't here before," thought the princess. "I wonder what sort of lock a key like this opens?"

The princess searched all over the gloomy castle, from the cellars to the roof. Then, in the attic, she found a chest made of ancient wood. The princess put the key in the lock and, when she turned it, the lock clicked open. Inside the chest was an old tin whistle.

The princess took the tin whistle to her room and tried to play it. She was surprised to find that her fingers flew over the holes and she was able to play a lovely tune. The princess stood up and danced round and round her room as she played.

Suddenly, as if by magic, the china ornaments in the princess' room started to twirl and dance along to the music. The princess was very surprised, but she didn't stop playing.

The princess danced down the stairs, playing the tune. The rusty suits of armour came to life and marched merrily behind her. Even the knives and forks in the kitchen began to beat in time to the music. Then the plates and cups began to dance together.

In the great hall, all the chairs danced in formation and even the long, oak table began to jig around. Inside the paintings, the princess' ancestors danced and twirled. Even the stuffed moose head on the wall began to sing along, cheerfully.

"What is this noise?" asked the king, as he came marching into the hall with the queen. He grabbed the tin whistle and suddenly, all the dancing stopped. The king put the whistle in a drawer. "We'll have none of this in my castle," he said and sent the princess off to bed.

That night, the princess had a dream that she was looking out of her bedroom window at the statue in the garden. The statue seemed to be pleading with her. "Set me free," it said. "If you do not wake me tonight, I will remain stone for another one hundred years."

The princess woke up, dressed quietly and then crept downstairs. The castle guards were dozing and she slipped past them without a sound. The princess found the tin whistle in the drawer, where the king had put it, then she crept out into the moonlit garden.

Everything was still and quiet outside. The princess walked along the paths, towards the quiet spot where the statue stood. She played softly on the tin whistle. The moonlight shone brighter and brighter on the statue of the young man and made it glow. The princess played faster and faster, until her fingers ached and she could hardly breathe.

Suddenly, the statue moved. It raised its hands and slowly, all the stone changed into living flesh. The young man stepped down from the statue and took the princess' hand.

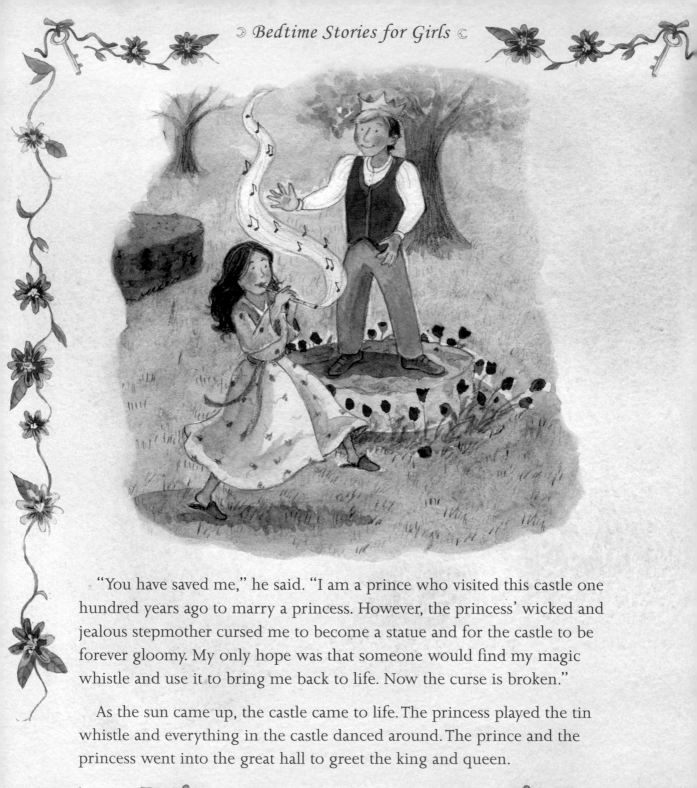

"You have saved me," he said. "I am a prince who visited this castle one hundred years ago to marry a princess. However, the princess' wicked and jealous stepmother cursed me to become a statue and for the castle to be forever gloomy. My only hope was that someone would find my magic whistle and use it to bring me back to life. Now the curse is broken."

As the sun came up, the castle came to life. The princess played the tin whistle and everything in the castle danced around. The prince and the princess went into the great hall to greet the king and queen.

The king and queen weren't unhappy anymore. In fact, they were overjoyed to see their daughter and the prince. They smiled and hugged each other. "We have lived under this enchantment for far too long," they said. "Now that the curse has been broken, we will make this castle a happy place once more."

The prince fell in love with the princess and it wasn't long before they were married. On the day of their wedding, everyone in the castle danced and danced. The castle was filled with light and laughter and no one had any reason to be unhappy, ever again.

Goldilocks and the Three Bears

Once upon a time, there were three bears who lived in a cottage in the woods. There was Father Bear, Mother Bear and Baby Bear. One day, Mother Bear made porridge for breakfast, but it was too hot to eat, so the bears decided to go for a walk until it cooled down.

Meanwhile, a little girl called Goldilocks was walking in the woods. It wasn't long before Goldilocks realised that she was lost. She wandered through the forest, trying to find her way home, but soon she became cold and hungry.

Goldilocks was feeling very fed up when she came upon the three bears' cottage. "Maybe someone lives here who can help me," she said. She went up to the little cottage and knocked on the door, but nobody answered. Goldilocks peered into a window, but she couldn't see anybody inside. So she tried the door and found it was open.

Goldilocks stepped inside the cottage. "Is anybody home?" she asked, but there was no reply because the three bears were still out on their morning walk. Goldilocks went to the kitchen and saw three bowls of porridge on the table. "I'm so hungry. I'm sure nobody will mind if I just have a taste," she thought to herself.

Goldilocks tasted the biggest bowl of porridge, but it was too hot.

So she tasted the middle bowl of porridge, but it was too cold.

Then Goldilocks tasted the smallest bowl of porridge and it was just right, so she gobbled it all up.

When Goldilocks had finished the porridge, her tummy felt really full. "I think I will find somewhere comfortable to sit down and have a rest," she said.

Goldilocks looked around and saw three chairs. The first chair was very big and Goldilocks found it hard to climb up onto the seat.

So, she tried the middle chair instead. It was a bit better, but it was still too high.

However, when Goldilocks tried the smallest chair, it seemed to be just right

Goldilocks sat back on the chair and was just getting comfortable when suddenly, the legs snapped and she fell to the floor.

"I'm sleepy," thought Goldilocks, so she went upstairs and found a bedroom with three beds in it. There was a big one, a medium-sized one, and a tiny little one.

Goldilocks jumped onto the biggest bed, but it was far too hard.

So, she tried sleeping on the middle-sized bed, but it was far too soft.

Goldilocks laid down on the smallest bed. It was just right, so she laid her head on the pillow and fell fast asleep.

Soon, the three bears finished their walk and returned to the cottage. They were surprised to see that the front door was open. They went into the kitchen and Father Bear looked at the big bowl. "Someone's been eating my porridge," he said.

Mother Bear looked at the middle bowl, which had a spoon sticking out of it. "Someone's been eating my porridge," she said.

Baby Bear looked at the small bowl. "Someone's been eating MY porridge," he said, "and they've eaten it all up!"

Father Bear went to sit down, but the big chair wasn't in its usual place. "Someone's been sitting in my chair," he said.

Mother Bear saw that the middle chair had been moved, too. "Someone's been sitting in my chair," she said.

Baby Bear looked at the small chair lying smashed on the floor. "Someone's been sitting in MY chair," he wailed, "and they've broken it to pieces!" Baby Bear started to cry.

The three bears went upstairs to their bedroom. Father Bear saw that the sheets had fallen off the biggest bed. "Someone's been sleeping in my bed," he said.

Mother Bear looked at the crumpled pillows on the medium-sized bed. "Someone's been sleeping in my bed," she said.

Baby Bear pointed at the smallest bed. "Someone's been sleeping in MY bed," he said, "and she's still there!"

Suddenly, Goldilocks woke up with a start. She sat up and saw the three bears looking down at her. With a shriek, she scrambled out of the bed, ran downstairs and out of the cottage, into the woods. She didn't dare look behind her, in case the three bears were following her, but the three bears were still in the bedroom, scratching their heads and wondering why a little golden-haired girl had gone to sleep in Baby Bear's bed.

Goldilocks ran so fast, she soon found herself back home again. She rushed in and hugged her mother who had been worrying where she was. After that, Goldilocks didn't go into the woods by herself and she never went back to the three bears' cottage again.

Rumpelstiltskin

Once upon a time, a king visited a humble miller. The miller longed to impress the king, so he boasted about his beautiful daughter. "My daughter is a very good spinner," said the miller. "She can spin straw into gold!"

The king was amazed to hear this. He ordered the miller's daughter to be locked in a tower in his castle. He left her there with a heap of straw and a spinning wheel. "You have three days to spin all this straw into gold," said the king. "If you fail, you will be punished."

But the poor miller's daughter couldn't really spin straw into gold. Her father had lied to the king and now she had been set an impossible task. The miller's daughter sat in the tower room and wept.

Suddenly, the stone wall of the tower seemed to ripple like water and a strange little man stepped through. He was short and had an ugly, bearded little face. "What's all this noise?" asked the man, grumpily. The miller's daughter explained her problem.

The little man stroked his hairy chin. "What will you give me if I spin this straw into gold?" he asked. The miller's daughter thought hard. "You can have my necklace," she said.

The man looked at the girl's necklace and nodded. He sat at the spinning wheel and began to spin. By morning, he had spun some of the straw into gold. Then, as quickly as he had arrived, the strange little man disappeared back into the wall.

The next morning, the king was pleased when he saw the gold, but he wanted more. "If the rest of the straw isn't spun into gold in two days, you will be punished," he said to the miller's daughter.

That night, the little man returned. "What will you give me if I spin you more gold?" he asked. The miller's daughter gave him her bracelet and the man spun more of the straw into gold.

When the king came to collect the gold the next morning, he was very happy. He thought the miller's daughter was beautiful and he almost told her to stop spinning, but he couldn't resist wanting more gold. "You must spin the remaining straw into gold tonight," he said.

That night, the miller's daughter waited and waited for the little man to appear. It was past midnight before the wall rippled and he stepped out. "Quick," she said. "You must spin the rest of the straw into gold, or I shall be in great trouble."

The little man grinned at her. "What will you give me if I do?" But the miller's daughter had nothing left to give to him.
"I will spin this straw into gold for you," said the man, "if you promise to give me your first-born child."

The miller's daughter was so frightened, she agreed. The little man sat at the wheel and worked faster than ever. Just as the sun came up, the last straw was spun into gold. The little man disappeared through the wall and the king opened the door.

The king was so amazed at the miller's daughter's skill and beauty that he asked her to marry him straight away. The miller's daughter agreed, as long as the king never asked her to spin gold into straw again.

The king was married to the miller's daughter and she became the queen. In time, she had a beautiful baby daughter. She had forgotten all about her promise until one day, the wall of her room rippled like water and the strange little man stepped out. "You made a promise to give me your first-born child," he said.

The queen hugged her baby tight and would not let her go. "Take all my riches instead," she pleaded.

"No!" snapped the little man in triumph. "Only those who know my name have power over me. You do not know my name, so I will take your baby and you cannot stop me."

"Wait," said the queen, trying to think quickly. "It took you three days to spin the straw, so I should have three days to guess your name."

"Very well," said the little man, "but in three days, your baby is mine!"

The next day, when the man reappeared, the queen tried all the names she could think of. The little man just laughed and said, "no," to every one that she suggested.

On the second day, the queen searched through every book in the castle's great library. There was nothing about a little man who could spin straw into gold. Once again, the cackling man appeared and then disappeared when the queen failed to guess his name.

On the morning of the third day, the queen was in despair at not being able to figure out the man's name. She took her baby out with her and walked for miles, through fields and forests.

Just as the queen was ready to give up, she saw a thin line of smoke, floating through the trees. Following it, she saw a funny little house. Outside the house, there was a small fire. The little man who had spun gold from straw was dancing around the fire, laughing and singing a strange song.

The queen crouched down by the trees and kissed her baby to make sure she made no noise. Then she listened to the little man's song.
"The queen's daughter I'll surely claim.
The queen can't beat me at my game.
Rumpelstiltskin is my name!"
The queen crept away and then rushed back to the castle as fast as she could.

Later that night, just as he had done before, the strange little man appeared. "Your time is up," he said. "The child is mine, so hand her over. I will take her to Fairyland and she will grow up to be my slave." The little man clapped his hands with glee.

"I have one last guess," said the queen. "I think that your name is Rumpelstiltskin."

When Rumpelstiltskin heard his name being spoken, he was enraged. His face was red with fury. He jumped up and down and stamped so hard on the ground, he made a great hole in it. Then he disappeared through the wall, still shouting and screaming with rage. After that, Rumpelstiltskin was never seen or heard of again.

The king and queen's daughter grew up to be a beautiful young woman. No one ever told her that she was once nearly spirited off to Fairyland and everyone lived happily ever after.

The Nightingale
and the North Wind

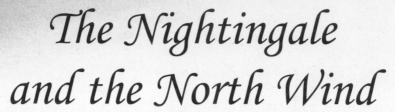

One windy evening, a little nightingale was singing her sweet, beautiful melody in a big horse-chestnut tree on a village green. The North Wind, the coldest and iciest of the four winds, blew so hard, it whistled through the leaves and shook the branches of the tree. The poor nightingale nearly fell off her branch and had to stop singing. "North Wind!" she cried. "Please stop all that blowing and whistling. I'm trying to sing."

The North Wind heard the nightingale. "Why should I, the mightiest of winds, stop blowing for you, little bird?" he asked.
"The answer to that question is a very simple one," said the nightingale. "You should stop blowing because my song is more powerful than your mighty breath."

The North Wind thought that this was most amusing. "Is that so?" he said. "In that case, would you care to make a bet?"
"Certainly," said the nightingale. "What are your terms?"

The North Wind thought for a moment. "We'll see who can make the most people in the village gather by this big tree," he said. "I'll go first and if I win, I will blow as hard as I like, forever. However, if you win, I agree to stop blowing altogether."
The nightingale agreed to the bet and flew off to a nearby bush to watch.

At first, the North Wind tried blowing the villagers who were out walking. However, even though he managed to blow a few of them towards the tree, most of the villagers were already inside, eating their dinner or getting ready for bed. As soon as the North Wind turned to blow at one villager, another one would seize their chance and run back inside.

The North Wind blustered and grumbled and then he had another idea. He blew at the tree as hard as he could. The branches and their big, long leaves swayed in the wind. The North Wind blew even harder, until the weather vane on top of the church whirled like a spinning top.

The people of the village peeped out of their windows and wondered what was happening. "It's strange weather for this time of year," they said, as they watched the wind blow through the village.

The North Wind blew so hard that a great branch of the horse-chestnut tree broke with a giant crack. It fell down onto the ground in a shower of leaves. "Now everyone in the village will come out to see," said the North Wind.

Some of the villagers rushed out to look at the broken branch, scratching their heads and complaining to each other about the awful weather. However, most of them stayed inside, fearful of the giant gusts of wind.

"Half the village must be out here," said the North Wind to the nightingale. "I'd like to see you do better."
The nightingale just nodded. "Wait until tomorrow night." she cheeped, cheerfully.

By the next evening, the villagers had cleared away the branch, fixed the thatch back onto their roofs and everything was back to normal.
The nightingale chose a much lower branch than usual and began to sing her wonderful song.

At first, the village green was empty. The North Wind who was looking on, laughed. "You see, nightingale," he hissed. "All your singing can't match my mighty breath."

The nightingale ignored him and just carried on singing her sweet, beautiful song. Nearby, a little girl was going home with her mother. "Listen," said the girl. "What a beautiful sound."

Soon, the mother began to listen to the nightingale's song, too. A man came and joined them. "What are you doing?" he asked. Then the man heard the nightingale singing and he stopped to listen as well.

Soon, more people began to stop to hear the nightingale's song.
The people in their houses wondered why their neighbours were gathering round the horse-chestnut tree and came to look.

The nightingale sang as loud and as beautifully as she could. Before long, the whole village had gathered around the horse-chestnut tree in wonder and delight.

"You win," said the North Wind. "You may be small, but your song really is more powerful than my mighty breath."

After that, the North Wind never blew around the horse-chestnut tree again and the nightingale sang sweetly to the villagers for many, happy years.